Extra Time

by

Jenny Oldfield

Illustrated by Maggie Downer

To my brother, Richard,
a football supporter

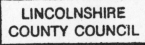

LINCOLNSHIRE
COUNTY COUNCIL

SCHOOLS

First published in Great Britain by Barrington Stoke Ltd
10 Belford Terrace, Edinburgh, EH4 3DQ
Copyright © 1999 Jenny Oldfield
Illustrations © Maggie Downer
The moral right of the author has been asserted in
accordance with the Copyright, Designs and
Patents Act 1988
ISBN 1-902260-13-9
Printed by BPC-AUP (Aberdeen) Ltd, Aberdeen
The publisher acknowledges subsidy from the Scottish Arts Council
towards the publication of this volume

THE SCOTTISH ARTS COUNCIL

MEET THE AUTHOR - JENNY OLDFIELD

What is your favourite animal?
A horse
What is your favourite boy's name?
Adam
What is your favourite girl's name?
Eve
What is your favourite food?
Crusty French bread
What is your favourite music?
Blues music
What is your favourite hobby?
Travelling

MEET THE ILLUSTRATOR - MAGGIE DOWNER

What is your favourite animal?
A field mouse
What is your favourite boy's name?
Sam
What is your favourite girl's name?
Jenny
What is your favourite food?
Chips
What is your favourite music?
Folk and traditional
What is your favourite hobby?
Dancing

Barrington Stoke was a famous and much loved story-teller. He travelled from village to village, carrying a lantern to light his way. He arrived as it grew dark and when the young boys and girls of the village saw the glow of his lantern, they hurried to the central meeting place. They were full of excitement and expectation, for his stories were always wonderful.

Then Barrington Stoke set down his lantern. In the flickering light the listeners were enthralled by his tales of adventure, horror and mystery. He knew exactly what they liked best and he loved telling a good story. And another. And then another. When the lantern burned low and dawn was nearly breaking, he slipped away. He was gone by morning, only to appear the next day in some other village to tell the next story.

Contents

Chapter 1
Danny and Ellie?

Danny knew he would never go out with Ellie Conner. He wasn't six feet tall with footballer's legs. His eyes weren't dreamy blue or drop-dead gorgeous brown. His legs were skinny and his eyes were plain grey.

Put it this way – Danny Dolan wasn't cool.

He did play football, though. Centre. When he scored a goal, he would jump and punch the air. The other kids would pile on top of him.

He'd come up muddy, fighting for breath. It was a good feeling. In fact, it was the best feeling in the world ... so far.

But he thought that going out with Ellie might beat scoring that winning goal.

"No way!" his older brother, Frankie, told him one Saturday night. "Girls are trouble. If you want my advice, you'll stick to soccer."

"I don't," Danny said. "Want your advice, that is." He sat on the sofa next to the family dog, Fred, and sulked his way through *Match of the Day*. He wished he hadn't breathed a word about Ellie.

"Please yourself." Frankie slammed the door on his way out to meet his girlfriend, Carli.

Carli Brown was Ellie's cousin. That would be a funny thing, Carli and Frankie, Ellie and Danny ... No chance!

Danny just couldn't get Ellie out of his mind. She darted into his head when he watched the match. Ellie in her blue school uniform, her long black hair swaying down her back. Ellie hanging out in the park, her big brown eyes turned away from the soccer pitch, showing she was bored ... She was probably at the disco right this minute. And here he was with his feet up, stuck in front of the telly.

Chapter 2
Ellie and Danny?

Ellie wondered if Danny Dolan would ever get round to asking her out.

"He's shy," her friend Annie told her at the disco. "You can tell by the way he looks at you that he wants to."

"He doesn't," Ellie sighed.

"What?" Annie asked.

" ... Look at me. Whenever he sees me coming, he looks the other way."

"Exactly!" Annie said, as if she'd proved a hard point. "Danny fancies you like mad. Trust me."

"No way!" Ellie went red. As red as the shirt Danny wore on the soccer pitch.

"Anyhow, even if he asked me I'd say no!"

Annie stared in the mirror at Ellie's blushing face. "If Danny Dolan asked you out, you'd say no?" she echoed.

"Yeah." It was time for them to get back to the music and the dancing. "Football is all Danny ever thinks about. That's where he probably is now, at home watching it on the telly!"

*****

But soft! what light through yonder window breaks?

Danny should have been watching a film with the rest of the class. Romeo was in love with Juliet. He hid in some bushes and watched her come out of her bedroom, going on about Juliet being as bright as the sun.

But Danny wasn't looking at the two on the video. He was staring at the back of Ellie's head. She wore her hair loose today. It swung and caught the light when she leaned sideways to whisper to her friend, Annie. It shone like silk. It was the colour of a blackbird's wing.

The teacher pressed the pause button. "Here Romeo is trying to explain how it feels to fall in love at first sight," he explained. "He thinks Juliet is like the sun and the stars rolled into one. He watches every move she makes."

Yeah, Danny thought. He caught sight of Ellie's face as she turned to stare out of the window. Her nose was short and turned up a bit at the end. He liked that shape of nose.

"But Romeo doesn't think he stands a chance with Juliet," the teacher droned on. "He thinks she's too far above him to notice him."

Yeah, Danny sighed. What would a gorgeous girl like Ellie be doing going out with an uncool kid like him?

The teacher pressed the play button.

It is my lady. O, it is my love!
O that she knew she were!

*****

"Shoot!" Annie yelled at Ellie.

She was Goal Attack for the blue team. Didn't they know she couldn't throw a stupid netball to save her life?

"Shoot!" the others yelled.

It was hot. The sun was in her eyes so she couldn't even see the basket. She held the ball in one hand and chucked it any old how.

It flew through the air, miles too high. It missed the basket and soared right over the netting. Bounce – bounce – bounce. Ellie's heart sank as she saw it land by Joey Watkins' feet, slap in the middle of the boys' soccer pitch.

"Great shot!" Joey laughed. He trapped the netball under his boot.

"Go and get it, Ellie!" The girls in her team wanted to get back at her for missing the shot.

"Yeah, Ellie, come and get your ball!" The boys were enjoying this.

"Go, Ellie!" Miss Carter ordered. "You're the one who threw it over."

She had to go down to the soccer pitch in her little pleated skirt, with her pale legs and red face. Joey still had his foot on the ball and a stupid grin all over his face. Danny Dolan and the rest of his team stood round gawping.

Ellie wished she could die. She wished a hole would open up in the middle of the pitch and swallow her. How long did she have to stand there before stupid Joey Watkins stopped grinning and handed over the stupid ball?

"Give her the ball, Joey," Danny muttered at last. He turned and pushed his way through the gawping gang. "Come on, let's get on with the game."

Chapter 3
Joey and Ellie?

Joey Watkins was six feet tall and he did have good legs. Danny thought he loved himself too much because of it. And now it looked like Joey fancied Ellie.

They were in the park that same night, kicking a ball around of course. Danny had brought Fred with him because Frankie said the dog shouldn't hang around the house so much. Fred kept running on to the pitch and trying to join in, which was fine except he didn't know the rules. Danny had to keep on grabbing him by the collar and dragging him off.

The girls, sitting on the low wall by the park gates, laughed every time. Ellie was there, looking brilliant. She shone out above the rest.

"Swee-eet!" Annie Lomax cooed at Fred.

The dog went and sucked up to her, poking his blunt, snotty nose against her legs. He wagged his stumpy tail.

"How do you rate my chances with Ellie Conner?" Joey asked anyone in the team who would listen. He stuck his chest out and mashed a smaller kid who got in his way in the goalmouth. He tooted the ball into the back of the net.

Milking the goal, Joey jumped and punched the air. The team went up to him and slapped him on the back. He did a victory jog past the wall where Annie, Ellie and the other girls sat.

"So go on, how do you rate my chances?" he asked Danny at the end of the game. His muscles bulged out of his T-shirt, his legs were definitely what girls would die for. "Shall I ask her to the next disco?"

Danny shrugged.

"Yeah, give it a go!" the other kids told him.

Everyone wanted to go out with Ellie, but none of them had the guts to ask. Except Joey.

Danny couldn't watch as Joey strolled over to the group of girls. He wanted to leave before anyone saw his miserable face. But Fred the dog let him down by trotting over to the girls.

"Here, Fred!" Danny whistled and called.

In the end he had to go and grab him by the collar as usual.

" ... So what do you think?" Joey was asking Ellie.

Ellie hid her face behind her long, black hair.

" ... Meet me outside the disco at half-seven tomorrow night," Joey said.

*****

Too late! Danny flung Fred's lead down on the floor. He stamped through the house and turned on the telly. There was no soccer on, just soaps and repeats. I waited too long and now it's too late!

"Who rattled your cage?" Frankie said, on his way out to see Carli.

Danny slammed the door in his face.

For months he'd wanted to ask Ellie out. He'd gone over and over it in his head. "Ellie, how would you like to come out with me?" "I was thinking, do you fancy seeing a film?" You never know, she might say yes. He'd go into school, winding himself up. It was going to be today. Today was the day when he would go up to Ellie in the corridor and ask her out. How many times had he said that? But he'd never had the guts.

And now Joey Watkins, the one with the legs, had gone ahead and done it. Tomorrow night at seven-thirty.

Danny groaned, turfed Fred the dog off the sofa, turned off the telly and went to bed.

Chapter 4
Drop-Dead Gorgeous

"What did you tell him?" Annie crowded Ellie into a corner early next morning. They stood by the lockers before registration.

"Come on, Ell, I heard Joey Watkins ask you to the disco. So what did you say?"

Ellie stuffed her bag into her locker. She enjoyed hearing the other girls gasp.

"Wow, Joey Watkins asked you out?"

"He's drop-dead gorgeous!"

"I wish he'd asked me!"

"You said yes, didn't you?" Annie opened her eyes wide and nodded her head.

Still Ellie didn't answer. She got out her copy of *Romeo and Juliet*, ready for English.

"So what will you wear?" Annie wanted to know. "I've got that white dress you could borrow, you know, the one with straps."

"No thanks." Ellie walked off down the corridor. It was fun to keep them guessing.

" ... Wow, Joey Watkins!"

" ... She seems pretty cool about it." The girls hung around by the lockers.

"Yeah, but really she's dead nervous." Annie led the gossip. "I know Ellie, she doesn't show it, but deep down she knows it's cool that she and Joey are an item."

Chapter 5
The Big Match

Man. United v. Juventus. It was the big match on cable TV, played out in front of an Italian crowd of 50,000. The players were warming up as the commentator explained about extra time, fifteen minutes each way if the tie ended in a draw. After that, a penalty shoot-out.

"It's just you and me, Fred," Danny told the dog. He'd grabbed the remote and switched on the telly, then stretched out full length on the

battered front-room sofa. He hadn't even bothered to change out of his crumpled school uniform.

To get comfy, Fred flopped down across Danny's chest. He wheezed and snuffled happily. A night in with Danny was OK by him.

"I'd rather watch the footie than go to some dumb disco," Danny said.

"Who are you trying to kid?" a voice inside his head demanded. "Ellie will be there out of school uniform, in a dress. She'll be the best looking girl in the room."

"If United win this, they'll be European Cup holders." Danny told Fred. The whistle went and the match kicked off – seven thirty on the dot.

The dog closed his eyes and snoozed.

"Ellie's meeting Joey right now, right this second," the voice in his head insisted. "They're going into the building. There's music, lights. Joey's asking her to dance. He's got his arm round her ..."

"United have to take the game to them," said Danny to Fred. He gritted his teeth. He had to concentrate on the football. "There's no point playing a defensive game against an Italian team. We have to attack."

On the TV screen the pitch looked superb, the twenty-two players were fit and fresh. He settled down to a battle of the giants.

Frankie put his head round the door fifteen minutes into the match.

"What's the score?"

"Still nil-nil. Why aren't you watching?"

"I'm off out with Carli. Keep an eye out for her, will you, while I have a quick shower. If she comes to the door, tell her I won't be long."

Frankie took off his T-shirt while he waited for a response. "Danny?"

"What? ... Yeah, yeah." The match was hotting up. Juventus had just caught United in the off-side trap and were now sweeping the ball back up the pitch, threatening the United goal. Danny sat up and yelled at the defence. For the next half an hour he was on the edge of his seat.

He was so busy telling his team what to do that he didn't hear the door bell ring.

"Danny!" Frankie yelled from the top of the stairs.

The half-time whistle went.

"Danny, get that, will you?"

Still no score. He took a deep breath. "Yeah, yeah," he told Frankie. But he went to the window first to check who was at the door.

Carli stood on tiptoe peering through the letter box and shouting, "Frankie, it's me!"

She wasn't alone. There was another girl standing with her back to the window. Danny recognised the long, blackbird-wing, glossy hair.

"Ellie!" he yelped.

On the sofa, Fred the dog opened one eye.

"Frankie!" Carli cried. "Open the door!"

Danny's brother stomped downstairs. "Thanks a lot, Dan!" he yelled through the closed front-room door.

Ellie! Here at his house. Not at the disco. Why not? What had happened to her date with the gorgeous Joey? Danny stared through the net curtain ... Ellie stepping over the doorstep, following Carli. Ellie in the hallway. Frankie saying "Hi!" to them both, telling them to wait in the front room.

"Danny's in there," Frankie explained as he went up to finish his shower. "He's watching the footie, but he won't mind two gorgeous girls like you interrupting him."

Mind? Danny saw the door handle turn. He was in a flat panic. Mind? He was in his school shirt and tie, his sock had a hole in the toe, for god's sake!

The door opened. The smell of perfume, hairspray and make-up wafted in.

Taking a run full pelt across the room, Danny jumped over Fred the dog and made a rugby dive down the back of the sofa.

*****

"Frankie's always late!" Carli sighed as she sat down beside Fred to wait. "I never let it bother me."

Ellie glanced round the room. The match was on TV, like Frankie said.

"As the teams come back onto the pitch for the second half, let's turn to our experts in the studio for a view of the match so far," the commentator said. "Does it look at this point as if we're heading for extra time, Alan?"

But there was no sign of Danny. Ellie frowned and sat on the sofa beside Carli, with Fred snuggled between them. The cushion sank sideways and tipped her off balance.

"You know men!" Carli went on. "They take ages to get ready. Shower, slap on the aftershave, change their clothes six times. Then, when they finally show up, you wonder what took them so long!"

"I thought you liked Frankie," Ellie reminded her.

"I do," Carli laughed. "But it doesn't stop me moaning at him when he's late. Anyway, what about you ... ? I heard you had a big date tonight."

*****

Danny lay flat on his stomach behind the sofa. He felt it sink and shift as the two girls sat down. There was fluff from the carpet up his nose. No one had hoovered behind here for years.

"Very clever!" the voice in his head said. "How come you're hiding behind your own sofa when the girl of your dreams is sitting on it?"

*****

Out there in the real world, the second half of the match was under way. Juventus were putting pressure on United's defence and the goalie put in a spectacular save.

*****

" ... Anyway, what about you?" Ellie's cousin, Carli, asked her. "I heard you had a big date tonight."

"Big date ... not!" Ellie told her. She patted Fred's head and kept on looking round the room. Where was Danny? Why wasn't he watching the match? "Unless you count Joey Watkins as the best thing since sliced bread, which I definitely do not."

*****

Danny's mouth dropped open. His jaw hit the carpet. Ellie didn't fancy Joey. Could this be true?

*****

"Isn't he the gorgeous one?" Carli got up from the sofa and went to turn down the volume on the TV. "And I heard he'd got a place on the county schoolboy soccer trials."

"So?" Ellie said.

"So why don't you want to go with him?"

"Because!"

She sat on the sofa and flicked her hair behind her shoulder. Ellie hadn't forgiven Joey for what he'd done to her during the netball game. He'd stood with his foot on her ball, making the other kids laugh. Danny had been the only one who didn't think it was funny,

"Ah, I get it!" Carli grinned. "You didn't go to the disco with Joey because you've got someone else!"

"No!" Ellie jumped in with a hot reply. It made Fred jump and struggle up into a sitting position. "If you must know, I haven't got a boyfriend at the moment."

"But you'd like one," Carli teased. "Yes you would, I can tell."

Chapter 6
Nil-Nil

Behind the sofa, Danny was in bits. He badly wanted to know the score in the match but Carli had turned the volume down. He wanted to know why Ellie didn't fancy Joey, but she wasn't saying. Most of all, he needed to find out why Ellie didn't have a boyfriend. Meanwhile, the dust from the carpet tickled the inside of his nose.

*****

"If you must know, I do like someone," Ellie confessed. "Only, I know he's never going to ask me out."

"Why not?" Carli was ready with advice. "You're a babe. I bet you can get anyone to go out with you if you try."

"He's too shy," Ellie sighed. "I've been giving him these signals that I like him for weeks now and he just ignores them."

"Like what for instance?"

"Like hanging round at school in the places I know he's going to be. Like going to the park in the evenings to watch him play footie, even though I hate the game."

Carli giggled. "Wash your mouth out with soap and water, Ellie Conner!"

"Well, I do! Anyway, I might as well not bother. It's like I'm invisible because all he ever thinks about is off-side rules, own-goals and extra time!"

*****

"Who is this dork?" Danny's inner voice said. "You mean to say some kid has got Ellie hooked and he's too dumb to notice?"

"I should be so lucky," Danny sighed. When he breathed in, he felt the sneeze build up. He pinched his nose tight and managed to stop it just in time.

*****

"So anyway, I'd never go out with him now," Ellie told Carli. "Even if he asked me, I'd say no!"

"Yeah, yeah!" Carli didn't believe a word. "Like, you fancy this kid for weeks and then you go off him just because he's obsessed with penalty shoot-outs. Well listen, so was Frankie until he met me!"

"Really?"

"Yeah, really." Carli stood up as the door opened and Frankie came in. "I was telling Ellie you were footie-mad until you started going out with me!"

Frankie went over to the TV and turned up the volume. "I still am. Like all us Dolans. What's the score?"

"Hey!" Carli turned it down again. "I thought we were going to rent a video?"

"Let me find out the score first." Frankie turned the TV up.

*****

"We're running into injury time, the referee's looking at his watch," the commentator said. "And the score is Juventus nil, Manchester United nil!"

Danny gave a silent groan. It meant they would have to play extra time.

*****

"Now can we go and rent a vid?" Carli pestered.

Frankie gave in. "Danny's recording the match anyway." He frowned and glanced round. "Hey, where is Danny anyway?"

"He wasn't here when we came in," Ellie told him. "The room was empty except for Fred."

The dog heard his name and cocked one floppy ear. He raised himself on his hind legs and peered over the back of the sofa.

"So you'll be OK here while we pop down for a vid?" Carli asked Ellie as she linked arms with Frankie and went out.

Ellie nodded. "Fine. I'll sit and watch the match."

*****

Danny turned his head to see Fred staring down at him. The dog's ears had flopped over his eyes. He snuffled and whined quietly.

Bang! The door closed behind Carli and Frankie. Ellie was alone in the room.

GET LOST, Fred! Danny mouthed the words and waved the dog away. Nightmare! Ellie was alone and he was still hiding behind his own sofa!

"The final whistle has gone!" the commentator announced as Ellie turned up the sound. "The teams will take a short breather before they go into extra time."

"Woof!" Fred the dog thought it was a game. Hide and seek. Danny had hidden. He'd sought and found. "Woof! Woof!"

"No!" Danny cringed and crouched lower. "Go away, Fred!"

"Here, boy! Here, Fred!" Ellie's voice came closer. She leaned against the back of the sofa and joined the dog. "What is it? What have you found?"

Danny swallowed hard, then looked up.

Ellie peered down at him. "Danny!"

"Erm! ... I mean ... I was just ... !" Fumbling, mumbling, stumbling to his feet, he stood up and faced her.

" ... Hiding!" she gasped.

Fred leaped at them both in tail-wagging, head-butting joy. Good game. Let's play again!

Danny's face was blazing, his palms felt sweaty. Ellie was trying not to laugh.

"This kid you'd never go out with, even if he asked," he mumbled. He dusted down his school trousers, jerked his tie loose around his neck.

Ellie opened her brown eyes wide and nodded.

Danny had to go for it. She'd probably say no, but he'd got nothing to lose.

"Was it me?" he asked.

She blushed and pushed her hair back from her face. "Yes."

"And was it true, you won't go out with me?"

"This is looking dangerous!" the commentator cried in the background. "Very, very dangerous for Juventus! United have six men up front … a lovely cross … a chance to score … !"

"No," Ellie said softly, almost too quiet to be heard. She looked at Danny with a shy, soft smile.

Fred shoved his broad nose between them, pleading to play more games. Danny ignored him.

"Goal!" the commentator yelled. "Juventus nil, Manchester United one in the tenth minute of extra time!"

Chapter 7
Extra Time

The lights flashed green, red, blue. The music thudded out across the dark room.

Danny danced with Ellie. Frankie danced with Carli. Frankie and Carli, Danny and Ellie. He wasn't dreaming. It was real. The dream had come true. Ellie's black hair swung across her face and brushed his shoulder.

Joey Watkins stood and watched. That made Danny feel extra good. Danny Dolan had brought

Ellie Conner to the disco and Joey Watkins had to stand there and watch. Cool.

Ellie's smiles were all for Danny. She'd brought him away from the match at the end of extra time. She'd spent weeks on this and now it was happening. Danny not thinking about football, thinking about her instead.

The music crashed around them, the lights flashed.

"What was the score?" someone yelled at Danny as they got crushed into a corner.

"One nil to United in extra time!" he yelled back. He was floating. This was heaven. Never let it stop.

Other Barrington Stoke titles available:-

What's Going On, Gus? by Jill Atkins 1-902260-10-4

Hostage by Malorie Blackman 1-902260-12-0

Ghost for Sale by Terry Deary 1-902260-14-7

Billy the Squid by Colin Dowland 1-902260-04-X

Kick Back by Vivian French 1-902260-02-3

The Gingerbread House by Adèle Geras 1-902260-03-1

Virtual Friend by Mary Hoffman 1-902260-00-7

Tod in Biker City by Anthony Masters 1-902260-15-5

Wartman by Michael Morpurgo 1-902260-05-8

Screw Loose by Alison Prince 1-902260-01-5

Lift Off by Hazel Townson 1-902260-11-2

If you would like more information about the **BARRINGTON STOKE CLUB**, please write to:- Barrington Stoke Club, 10 Belford Terrace, Edinburgh, EH4 3DQ or visit our website at:- www.barringtonstoke.co.uk